HEIDI HECKELBECK

Is So Totally Grounded!

By Wanda Coven
Illustrated by Priscilla Burris

LITTLE SIMON
New York London Toronto Sydney New Delhi

LITTLE SIMON
An imprint of Simon & Schuster Children's Publishing Division
1230 Avenue of the Americas, New York, New York 10020
First Little Simon paperback edition September 2018
Copyright © 2018 by Simon & Schuster, Inc.
Also available in a Little Simon hardcover edition.
All rights reserved, including the right of reproduction in whole or in part in any form. LITTLE SIMON is a registered trademark of Simon & Schuster, Inc., and associated colophon is a trademark of Simon & Schuster, Inc. For information about special discounts for bulk purchases, please contact Simon & Schuster Special Sales at 1-866-506-1949 or business@simonandschuster.com. The Simon & Schuster Speakers Bureau can bring authors to your live event. For more information or to book an event contact the Simon & Schuster Speakers Bureau at 1-866-248-3049 or visit our website at www.simonspeakers.com.
Designed by Ciara Gay
Manufactured in the United States of America 0520 MTN
10 9 8 7 6 5 4 3
Library of Congress Cataloging-in-Publication Data
Names: Coven, Wanda, author. | Burris, Priscilla, illustrator.
Title: Heidi Heckelbeck is so totally grounded / by Wanda Coven ; illustrated by Priscilla Burris. | Description: First Little Simon paperback edition. | New York : Little Simon, 2018. | Series: Heidi Heckelbeck ; 24 | Summary: Having decided housecleaning is too much for her to handle, Heidi Heckelbeck pulls out her *Book of Spells* and conjures up a helper, with disastrous results. | Identifiers: LCCN 2017056688 | ISBN 9781534426443 (pbk) | ISBN 9781534426450 (hc) | ISBN 9781534426467 (eBook) | Subjects: | CYAC: House cleaning—Fiction. | Magic—Fiction. | Witches—Fiction. | Family life—Fiction. | Behavior—Fiction.
Classification: LCC PZ7.C83393 Hjm 2018 | DDC [Fic]—dc23
LC record available at https://lccn.loc.gov/2017056688

CONTENTS

Chapter 1

THE MEAN CLEAN

Heidi circled Friday the tenth on her Baby Animals calendar. *Only FIVE days until we get to see the movie,* Tristan and the Magical Toy Factory! Heidi Heckelbeck and her friends Lucy Lancaster and Bruce Bickerson had waited for it to come out for months.

They must have watched the trailer a hundred times.

Heidi hung her calendar back on her bulletin board and went down-stairs to see if anything fun was going

on. As she passed the living room, she noticed the vacuum cleaner was out.

Not a good sign. Then she stepped into the kitchen and saw a mop, a bucket, and Mom standing on a step stool, scrubbing the inside of a cupboard.

Oh no, Heidi thought. *It must be time for the Mean Clean!* The Mean Clean was Heidi's family's special cleanup day—and it always came without warning. During the last Mean Clean, Heidi had found a wet bathing suit in her dirty clothes pile. It had been sitting there for a whole week,

and her clothes had smelled *super-duper* gross. She had never left her dirty clothes in a pile again.

Maybe I can sneak out of here before Mom sees me, Heidi thought. She turned around and began to tiptoe out of the kitchen. But Mom already knew she was there. It was like she had eyes in the back of her head.

"And where do you think you're going?" Mom asked.

Heidi froze. "Um, *nowhere*?"

Mom climbed down from the step stool. "Good!" she said. "Because today is the Mean Clean. And I'd like *you* to clean the den."

Heidi moaned. This wasn't what she'd had in mind for her Sunday afternoon. Then she remembered one of the best rules of the Mean Clean: find-ers keepers. *Hmm,* she thought. *Maybe I'll find some lost treasure under the couch cushions.*

"Okay," agreed Heidi as she rolled up her sleeves. She was ready to get to work.

COUCH TREASURE

Heidi grabbed a fistful of rags, along with some all-purpose cleaner, a feather duster, a lint roller, a pair of rubber gloves, and a trash bag.

"Look out, dirty den—here I come!" she said, setting down her cleaning supplies. Then she got the vacuum from the living room and pulled it behind her. That's when her little brother, Henry, showed up.

"I get dibs on the den!" he said.

"Oh no," Heidi said as she pointed

to the door. "Scramoosh! I got dibs FIRST. Mom's orders."

But Henry wouldn't leave. He ran to the couch and tugged on one of the cushions. Heidi pushed her brother aside and sat on the cushion.

"HEYYYYYY!" Henry complained, reaching for the next cushion. "What do you think you're DOING?"

Mom heard them and appeared in the doorway.

"Drop the cushion, Henry," she said. "I asked Heidi to clean the den."

Henry let go of the cushion and looked at Mom. "But you gave her the den *last* time," he complained.

Heidi did a little victory wiggle.

"That's true, Henry, but your room is the messiest," Mom said. "And I want you to clean it up."

Henry stuck out his lower lip. "But I already *know* what's in my room," he said. "And I'd much rather see what's under the couch cushions."

Mom pointed to the second floor, and Henry trudged upstairs.

After that, Heidi got right to work. She was anxious to see what was hidden in the couch cushions too. Some lost treasure, she hoped.

As Heidi slowly removed the first seat cushion, she saw a quarter. Then she spied another! She also found a dime, two nickels, and three pennies. She counted seventy-three cents total. *Jackpot!*

She moved to the next cushion and found Henry's yellow yo-yo, a pen, some lint, and a library card. *Not bad,* she thought. Under the next cushion she found a glob of homemade slime, which was as hard as a rock—and

pretty gross. She slid a rubber glove on and

peeled the slime away from the fabric. Then she picked the rest of it off with her fingers.

One more cushion to go, Heidi said to herself. She stared at it hopefully. Maybe she'd find something great, like a twenty-dollar bill.

But when she lifted the cushion, all she found was a smelly apple core, some stale popcorn, and—*YUCK*—somebody's fingernail clippings!

"*EEEEEEEEWWWWWWWW!*"
Heidi screamed, and then she ran
as fast as she could up to her room.
Sometimes buried treasure should
just stay buried.

Chapter 3

HELLO, DUSTY!

Heidi shut her bedroom door. This cleaning job was way too big and too *gross* for her to do all by herself.

I need a helper! Heidi thought as she pulled her *Book of Spells* out from under the bed. She found a spell for a little housekeeping help.

How to Clean Everything!

Have you ever found a rotten apple core underneath your couch cushions? Do you have an army of dust bunnies hiding beneath your bed? Perhaps you have a nasty ring of soap scum around your bathtub? If you're tired of a dirty, messy house and could use a little housekeeping helper, this is the spell for you!

Ingredients:

1 dirty sock

3 strands of hair

1 paper towel

1 pump of hand soap

Place the ingredients in a bowl and squish them together five times.

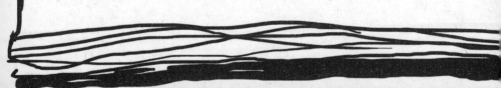

Hold your Witches of Westwick
medallion in your hand, and place
your other hand over the mix.
Then chant the following words:

DUSTER, MOPPER, SCRUBBER, SWEEPER!

THAT'S WHAT MAKES A GOOD HOUSEKEEPER!

LISTEN NOW TO MY COMMAND—

PLEASE SEND ALONG A HELPING HAND!

1. In a spell that calls for hair, a witch must always use
her own hair—or it will cause magical mistakes. 2. A witch
must also always thank the housekeeper for a job well done.

Heidi went to collect the ingredients. A dirty sock was easy to find. It was also very stinky. Paper towels were everywhere, but Heidi's hairbrush was nowhere to be seen in all the mess. So she snuck into the bathroom and borrowed Henry's brush.

What's the big deal? Heidi thought. *Hair is hair!* She pulled three hairs from the brush and added them into the mix.

After that Heidi squirted in the soap and squished the ingredients together five times. Then she held her medallion and put her hand over the bowl while she chanted the spell.

POOF!

There, standing before her, was a very unusual orange creature. It looked like an oversize fur ball with beady little eyes and a snaggletooth smile.

Heidi gasped. "Wow! You don't look anything like I thought you would!"

"What were you expecting?" the creature asked. "Fairy wings? Not all helpers have magic wands, you know."

Heidi blushed. "Oh, I'm sorry. I don't care what you look like. I'm just thrilled to have a helper. My name is Heidi. What's your name?"

The fluffy orange housekeeper smiled and spun in a circle. He was actually kind of adorable.

"I'm Dusty!" he said. "And I'm here to help you clean. Do you have a job for me?"

Heidi grinned from ear to ear. "Well, *HELLO,* Dusty!" she said. "Do I have a job for YOU!"

Chapter 4

THE DUSTBUSTER

"How about you start with my bed-room?" Heidi said.

Dusty got right to work and cleaned like a whirlwind. He folded Heidi's clothes and put them away. He lined up her shoes and dusted everything with his fuzzy fur! He shelved her books, including her *Book of Spells*, and used his hands to vacuum the rug and curtains.

"All done!" Dusty said. "What should I clean next?"

Heidi clapped her hands. *This is FUN!* she thought. *I could get used to having a cleaning assistant.*

"Now I want you to clean the den," she said, forgetting to say thank you for cleaning her room. "But let's play a game and make sure *nobody* sees you."

Heidi knew that Mom and Dad would not be happy if they found out she was using her witching powers to get out of the Mean Clean.

Then he bobbed his head and raced downstairs to the den. Heidi was right behind him. As he went to work she sat in Dad's easy chair and put her feet up to relax.

This is the life, she thought. Heidi imagined all the jobs she could give Dusty to do. *Why didn't I get a magical helper sooner?*

Just as she was getting excited about her new future with Dusty, a loud noise rattled Heidi back to reality.

Clickety-clickety click vroom! Dusty's vacuum arms roared to life and sucked up Henry's marble collection, followed by Mom's knitting yarn and Dad's socks. He even sucked up all of Heidi's precious *loot* that she'd found in the couch cushions.

"HEY! WAIT!"
Heidi   warned.
"Take it easy!"

But something

was wrong. Dusty

did not slow down at all. Instead, he

was speeding up! He began to throw

away all the wrong things. He tossed

Henry's favorite comic books into the

wastebasket with a *klunk*. He threw

Mom's favorite throw pillows into the fireplace. He even chucked Dad's deck of cards out the window.

Heidi covered her mouth as she watched the cards scatter into the yard. *Dusty's gone BONKERS! I'd better fix this, and FAST!*

She grabbed the comic books out of the wastebasket and put them back on the shelves. Then she rescued

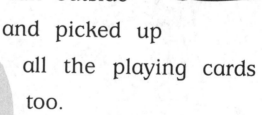

Mom's throw pillows from the fireplace, which, thankfully, was clean! She ran outside and picked up all the playing cards too.

"Merg!" Heidi cried as she came back into

the room. "What are you doing NOW?"

Dusty held a paintbrush and was about to zigzag it up and down the walls.

"No! Don't paint anything, Dusty!" Heidi grabbed the paintbrush. It was covered in bright pink paint. "Maybe just keep vacuuming, but please be careful."

Dusty nodded and said, "Okay."

Heidi snuck into the kitchen to hide Dusty's paintbrush before it dripped on the floor. *If Mom and Dad see this, I will be in so much trouble!* she thought. Luckily, her parents were downstairs, cleaning the basement.

Just as Heidi put the paintbrush in the trash, she heard Dusty's arm vacuum start again.

When she came back
into the den, she couldn't
see Dusty anywhere. Then
she looked up, and there
was Dusty—vacuuming
the ceiling.

Heidi chased the little orange helper
back and forth. Finally she grabbed
ahold of his legs and yanked.

Kabonk! Dusty tumbled onto the floor and instantly coughed out everything he had vacuumed up! The marbles rolled around the

room. Dad's socks stuck to the ceiling fan. Worst of all, Mom's yarn softly bumped into a glass vase. Heidi watched as the vase wobbled in slow motion on the side table, then tipped over.

CRASH!

And everything in the house went quiet.

47

Chapter 5

SHATTERED

Heidi stared helplessly at the broken glass. The rest of the room was a mess too. Dirt, lint, hair, and crumbs were everywhere. Heidi even spied one of the quarters that Dusty's vacuum had eaten. Then she heard footsteps pounding up the basement stairs.

"What's going on?" Mom called out. Dusty disappeared at the sound of Mom's voice.

"Everything's fine," Heidi answered. "Except for this vase."

"Oooooh!" Mom cried when she saw the room. Then she put her hands against her cheeks. "My beautiful hand-blown vase! It's *ruined*!"

Heidi didn't know what to do, so she dropped to her knees and tried to fit some of the shards together, like a puzzle.

"Heidi, *stop*!" Mom snapped. "You might cut yourself!"

Heidi dropped the pieces of glass, and they shattered even more.

 "I'm so sorry, Mom." The tears welled up in Heidi's eyes. "I was cleaning and things got a little out of control."

Mom sighed and shook her head. "Did you know that vase was an antique? It's been in the family for *two* generations. I was going to hand it down to *you* one day."

Heidi stared at the splintered remains of the vase on the floor. "I'm really sorry . . . ," she said. Her sniffles grew louder.

Mom knelt on the floor beside Heidi. "That vase meant a lot to me," she said. "You should've been more careful."

Heidi rubbed the tears from her cheek. "But I didn't mean to."

Mom nodded her head sadly. "I know you didn't *mean* to, but I'm afraid I'm going to have to ground you for the next *two* weeks. Now please go to your room."

Heidi moaned and left the den without another word.

Chapter 6

SOMETHiNG SNAPPED

Henry popped out of his bedroom and followed Heidi down the hall.

"I heard everything," he said. "You're in SO much trouble."

Heidi muttered something *not nice* under her breath.

"What did you just say?" Henry

asked. "I couldn't *hear* you!"

Heidi whipped around and faced her brother. "I said, *I hope your room NEVER gets clean!*"

No sooner had the words come out of her mouth than Heidi saw an orange, furry blur dash into Henry's room. *Uh-oh,* she thought. *Dusty!*

"That's a GOOD ONE!" Henry said to his sister. "Because—FOR YOUR INFORMATION—my room is ALREADY spotless."

Heidi sniffed and walked away from her brother, but Henry followed her down the hall.

"Don't you wanna see my perfectly clean room?" he asked.

Heidi stopped and turned around. "No," she said nervously. She didn't want to imagine what Dusty might have done to Henry's room.

"You're just jealous because I'm better at cleaning than you!" Henry bragged.

"Okay then," Heidi said with a knowing smirk. "Let's see what you've got."

They walked back to her brother's room. Henry opened the door and gasped.

"WHAT HAPPENED?" he cried, falling to his knees. Heidi had to admit, Henry's room looked a lot worse than she had expected.

His clothes hung out of open dresser drawers. A pair of under- wear drooped from his bedpost. Toys, books, smashed potato chips, and stuffed animals had been flung every which way. And, of course, Dusty was nowhere to be seen.

"Nice work!" Heidi told her brother. "But I gotta go!" Then she bolted back to her room while poor Henry sat on the floor with his head in his hands.

I have to reverse this Dusty spell before he destroys the whole house! Heidi thought. She opened her *Book of Spells.*

"Ahem," someone said behind her. Heidi looked up to see Mom, arms folded, standing in the doorway.

"Hand it over." Mom extended one hand. "Magic isn't going to get you out of *this* one."

Heidi reluctantly gave the book to Mom.

"Wait, Mom," Heidi complained. "You don't understand. . . ."

Mom tucked the *Book of Spells* under her arm. "No magic. You're grounded—remember?"

Heidi rolled her eyes. Like, how could she forget?

"I know. I know," Heidi mumbled.

Mom leaned against the doorframe and asked, "Do you understand what being grounded means?"

Heidi had never been grounded before, so she wasn't exactly an expert. She shook her head.

"It means no magic, no friends, no screens, and no leaving the house for two weeks except to go to school. Do you understand?"

Heidi nodded.

"Now you have my permission to leave your room and get back to cleaning," Mom said as she turned to go. "And why don't you help your brother? He seems to be having some trouble cleaning his room."

"Yes, ma'am," Heidi said.

As soon as her mom walked away, Dusty burst out of the closet.

Heidi fixed her eyes on the little helper.

"There you are," she said angrily. "I have NO THANKS for you."

Dusty took two steps back. The words "no thanks" hit him like a punch in the stomach.

"Furthermore," Heidi went on, "you're a BAD helper. You've done nothing but get me in trouble!"

As she spoke, Dusty furrowed his brows. He narrowed his eyes and balled his fists.

And then something inside him SNAPPED.

71

Chapter 7

DUSTY DESTRUCTO

There was no other way to describe it: Dusty went wild. He zoomed to the bathroom and made a monstrous mess. He squirted toothpaste on the mirror, poured bubble bath in the toilet, and pumped hand soap all over the sink.

Then Dusty grabbed a roll of toilet paper and ran down the hall, leaving a long ribbon behind him.

Heidi smacked the palm of her hand against her forehead and cried, "What have I done now?"

She chased after Dusty and tried to pick up the messes he left in his path.

The linen closet door flew open. Dusty pulled out all the towels and draped them over the banisters. Then he shook a giant box of cotton balls and Heidi watched the white fluffs drift down like snow. When she looked up, Dusty was gone.

Now where is he? Heidi wondered. She heard banging coming from the laundry room and followed the sound. Dusty had pulled all the laundry out of the washer. As Heidi picked up the wet clothes, Dusty shook a whole container of soap pods onto the floor. He began to stomp on them. *Splat! Sploosh! Splurp!* The bright blue-and-green soap splattered the walls and the floor.

When he was done messing up that room, Dusty raced into the hall and slid down the stairs.

"STOP!" Heidi yelled, tearing after him. But Dusty zoomed on through the kitchen, knocking over a full jug of milk on the kitchen table. Then— *whoosh!*—he slipped out the back door. Heidi stopped just as she was about to bump smack into Dad, who was coming in from taking out the trash.

"Not so fast," Dad said.

Heidi froze. *Did Dad see Dusty?*

"I believe you are grounded," Dad said, "which means no leaving the house."

Heidi turned around. Then Dad pointed to the overturned jug of milk, which was still dripping onto the floor.

"Did you spill all that milk?" her father asked.

Heidi laughed nervously. "*Wellll,* I think I may have bumped into the table by accident when I was passing by." She looked timidly at her father.

Dad did not look happy. "Please
wring out the sponge and clean up
the milk," he said.

Heidi went to the sink. She took the sponge, ran water over it, and squeezed it. Outside the window, Heidi could see Dusty scrambling down the driveway and away from the house.

Oh, phew, phew, and DOUBLE phew! Heidi thought. *Now Dusty can be somebody else's problem!*

Chapter 8

MYSTERY MESS

Heidi skipped happily down the hall to her classroom the next morning. All the messes at home had been picked up, and Dusty had not returned. Everything was finally back to normal—that is, until Heidi noticed a crowd gathered in the hallway.

Melanie Maplethorpe,
Stanley Stonewrecker,
and Bryce Beltran
were standing
nearby.

"What's going
on?" Heidi asked.

Melanie turned
and looked Heidi up
and down. "Oh, didn't you hear?" she
said in her oh-so-snooty way.

"The school is about to
give you an award,
and we're all here to
celebrate."

Heidi raised an eyebrow and looked at Bryce and Stanley for more information.

Bryce laughed and waved Melanie off. "She's only joking. We have no idea what's going on. Principal Pennypacker asked everyone to wait here in the hall."

Heidi nodded. *Wait for what?* she wondered. She really wanted to know what was going on. The crowd was directly outside her classroom. Heidi stood up tall to get a better look inside, but there were too many kids blocking the door.

"SHHHHHHH," somebody warned. "Principal Pennypacker's coming!"

The principal opened the door and stepped into the hall.

"Good morning, children," he began. "Everything is okay, but today Mrs. Welli's class will meet for art in Mr. Doodlebee's room. Everyone, that is, except for Heidi Heckelbeck. Could I speak with you alone, Heidi?"

Heidi blushed. *Why did the principal call me out in front of the WHOLE class?* she wondered. *This is SO embarrassing!*

And to make matters worse, her classmates all stared at her as they shuffled off to art.

Principal Pennypacker ushered Heidi into the classroom. Her teacher Mrs. Welli was standing beside Heidi's desk, which had been turned upside down. Heidi's books and school supplies were spilled all over the floor. Heidi's cubby had been raided too.

Her polka-dot rain boots were lying on Mrs. Welli's desk, and her lime-green lunch containers were on top of the guinea pig cage. Even her dirty gym clothes were draped over her classmates' desks and chairs.

"Heidi," said Mrs. Welli in a gentle tone, "did you make this mess?"

Heidi shook her head.

"Perhaps there's something you want to tell us?" asked Principal Pennypacker.

Heidi looked at her teacher and the principal. *Hey!* she thought. *They think I did this!*

"Wait," Heidi declared. "You've got it all wrong! I PROMISE I did not do any of this."

Principal Pennypacker looked at the classroom. "Can you think of any other way this might have happened, Heidi?"

It's totally my magical mess-maker Dusty's fault, Heidi wanted to say, but she could never admit that to her teacher and the principal.

Instead, she tried to get out of this weird situation as quickly as possible. "Would it be okay if I cleaned everything and joined my class in art?"

Principal Pennypacker looked at Mrs. Welli and nodded. Then they stepped into the hall to talk privately.

Heidi sighed and began to pick up the mess. As she collected her things she heard someone giggle. She looked over and saw Dusty hiding behind the fish tank. He'd been spying on Heidi the whole time.

"Okay, Dusty. Enough is enough," she declared as he ran away. "If it's a mess you want, then it's a mess you'll get."

97

Chapter 9

SO MESSED UP

When Heidi got home from school, she grabbed a box of Oaty-O's and a family-size bag of potato chips and ran up to her room. *Maybe if I make a huge mess, Dusty will go back to cleaning—instead of making messes,* Heidi reasoned. *Then again, maybe*

we're both just com-
pletely crazy.

Heidi shut the
door and began
to mess up her
room—*big time*.
She pulled all of her
clothes out of the drawers
and flung them all over the place.

She unloaded her
bookshelf and
scattered her
books, toys,
and stuffed
animals

across the floor. She tipped over her wastebasket, her pencil cup, and the laundry hamper. Finally she dumped the Oaty-O's and potato chips all over the floor.

CRUNCH!
SCRUNCH!
CRUNCH!
SCRUNCH!
She walked over the cereal and chips, mashing them into the carpet.

When she was done, Heidi stood back and admired the mess. *If Mom sees this, she'll ground me through middle school!* But Heidi didn't care. She had to catch Dusty.

She also needed
to get back her
Book of Spells.
She snuck into
Mom and Dad's
room, grabbed the

book off Mom's dresser,
then she ran back to her room and
hid under her bed to read her book.
This is an emergency, she told herself.

She had to find out two things: What had gone wrong with the spell? And how could she make Dusty disappear?

While she waited for Dusty, Heidi looked up the How to Clean Everything! spell. This time she read the fine print, which she had overlooked before.

1. *In a spell that calls for hair, a witch must always use her own hair— or it will cause magical mistakes.*

Heidi had used Henry's hair in the spell! *So that's why Dusty is so annoying!*

2. *A witch must also always thank the housekeeper for a job well done.*

"That has to be why Dusty went bananas," Heidi whispered. "I never thanked him for his help!"

Wham! The door banged open.

Heidi peeked out from under the bed and saw Dusty skittering inside. He studied the chaos and rubbed his hands together.

"Now, this is a perfectly wonderful mess!" he cried. "Just the kind I like to clean up!"

Dusty got right to work. He tidied, dusted, swept, vacuumed, and organized, and he even folded all the clothes and put them away again. Heidi's room was spotless! Her plan had worked. Making a mess had caused

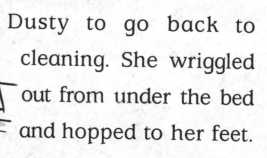

Dusty to go back to cleaning. She wriggled out from under the bed and hopped to her feet.

"Thank you for a job WELL DONE!"
she declared.

Dusty was surprised, but he smiled
broadly. She could tell that her thanks
meant a lot to him. "You're welcome,
Heidi!" he said.

And—*POOF!*—Dusty
vanished in a cloud
of sparkles. He even
returned the *Book of
Spells* to her mother's room.

Heidi let out a really *looong* sigh
and flopped onto her freshly made
bed, which smelled like flowers. Had
he washed everything in her room
too?

I did it! Heidi thought. *My troubles are over, except for one thing. I'm still grounded. MERG.*

Chapter 10

A FAMILY HEIRLOOM

The phone rang that evening.

"It's for you, Heidi," Mom said, handing her the telephone.

Heidi held it in front of her and pressed the speaker button.

"Hello?" she said.

"Hey, it's Bruce. My mom wants to

talk with *your* mom about a ride to the movies tomorrow night."

Heidi covered the receiver and looked at her mother. Mom shook her head and whispered, "Sorry, no movies. Remember, you're still grounded."

Super-merg, Heidi growled to herself. *What a mess I've made of everything!*

She had used magic for a job she should've done. She had forgotten to thank Dusty for helping her—and then he went loopy and broke Mom's vase. Now she had to let down her friends too.

"I'm really sorry," Heidi said, "but I can't go tomorrow night. I'm kind of grounded."

Bruce was quiet for a moment.
"That's too bad, Heidi," he said.
"But don't worry—the movie will still
be great after you're un-grounded!"

Heidi smiled. Only a true friend would forgive her for messing up the plan. She said good-bye to Bruce and hung up. Then she handed the phone back to her mother, who was looking at the table where the vase had been. Suddenly Heidi had an idea.

"Hey, Mom? Maybe we could shop for a new vase this weekend," Heidi suggested. "A hand-blown one that you can give to me when I grow up?"

Mom looked at Heidi and grinned. "Now, that's a wonderful idea," she said as she pulled Heidi close to give her a hug. And even though Heidi was still grounded, all was well at the Heckelbeck house.

Check out the next book starring HEIDI HECKELBECK

"Roar!"

"ROAR!"

"ROARRR!"

Heidi and Lucy squealed and hid underneath one of the picnic tables on the playground. Heidi's class was playing Cheese Dinosaur Tag, and Stanley Stonewrecker was the dinosaur. The rest of the class—or, at

An excerpt from *Heidi Heckelbeck Lights! Camera! Awesome!*

least, those who were playing—was the cheese. And, of course, in this game the dinosaur *loves* cheese and won't stop until he gets some.

"He'll never find us under here," Lucy whispered.

Heidi plunked onto the ground and accidentally bumped into a pair of pink polka-dot flats under the table. Heidi stared fearfully at the shoes because she knew exactly who they belonged to—Melanie Maplethorpe, her least favorite girl in the class.

Melanie peered under the table and glared at Heidi. "What do you think

An excerpt from *Heidi Heckelbeck Lights! Camera! Awesome!*

you're doing?" she cried, pushing the toe of her shoe into Heidi's side.

"Sorry," said Heidi as she dragged out the word like *saw-ree*.

Then Lucy noticed Melanie had a magazine in her hand.

"What are you reading?" asked Lucy, trying to change the mood under the table.

Melanie turned the magazine around so Lucy and Heidi could see the cover.

"I'm reading *She-She Magazine*," Melanie said, lightening up. "It's my absolute favorite."

An excerpt from *Heidi Heckelbeck Lights! Camera! Awesome!*